THE HOUND
OF THE
BASKERVILLES

ARTHUR CONAN DOYLE

REAL READS

www.realreads.co.uk

Retold by Tony Evans
Illustrated by Felix Bennett

Published by Real Reads Ltd
Stroud, Gloucestershire, UK
www.realreads.co.uk

Text copyright © Tony Evans 2011
Illustrations copyright © Felix Bennett 2011
The right of Tony Evans to be identified as author of
this book has been asserted by him in accordance with the
Copyright, Design and Patents Act 1988

First published in 2011

ISBN 978-1-906230-49-4

Printed in Malta by Gutenberg Press Ltd
Designed by Lucy Guenot
Typeset by Bookcraft Ltd, Stroud, Gloucestershire

CONTENTS

THE CHARACTERS

Sherlock Holmes

The famous and brilliant private detective. Will he be able to solve the terrifying mystery of the hound

Dr Watson

Sherlock Holmes' friend, dependable and brave. What strange discoveries will he make in Devonshire?

Sir Henry Baskerville

Sir Henry has inherited the Baskerville Estate. He is willing face any danger. But will his go fortune end in disaster?

4

Dr Mortimer

A young country doctor who examines the first victim. Will his evidence help to prevent another tragic death?

Mr Stapleton

...ever butterfly collector who lives near ...skerville Hall. What does he know ...ut the frightening creature that stalks the moor?

Miss Stapleton

Miss Stapleton is a fascinating and beautiful woman. Why is she so afraid?

Barrymore

Barrymore has been the faithful butler at Baskerville Hall for many years. What guilty secret is he hiding?

THE HOUND OF THE BASKERVILLES

Sherlock Holmes reached across the breakfast table for the silver-plated coffee pot.

'Our visitor should be arriving soon, Watson,' he said to me. 'I wonder what problem Dr Mortimer will bring for us?'

The doorbell rang and our housekeeper showed a young gentleman into the room. He was very tall and thin, with a long nose like a beak, which jutted out between two sharp, grey eyes, set closely together and sparkling brightly from behind a pair of gold-rimmed glasses.

'Dr Mortimer, allow me to introduce you to my friend and colleague, Dr Watson,' said Holmes. 'Do sit down, and please let me take your walking stick.'

As I poured Dr Mortimer a cup of coffee, Holmes took out his magnifying glass and looked closely at the heavy cane. 'Have you left your dog at home today, Sir?' he asked.

Our visitor looked up in surprise. 'He is downstairs with your housekeeper, Mr Holmes. But how did you know that I keep a dog?'

Holmes smiled. 'Elementary, Dr Mortimer. My reasoning is simple. The marks of your dog's teeth are very plainly visible on your stick. He has clearly been in the habit of carrying it for his master. But perhaps you would now be good enough to explain why you have called upon me today?'

Dr Mortimer looked anxiously at Holmes. 'It is a difficult problem to explain. As you know, I work as a family doctor in a wild and remote part of Dartmoor, near Baskerville Hall. If you will allow me, I would like to start with an ancient legend from that place.'

Holmes agreed, and Dr Mortimer began his story. 'The legend is believed to date from the time of Charles I, over two hundred and fifty years ago. The Baskerville estate was at that time held by Sir Hugo Baskerville, by all accounts a wild and godless man. One dark and

stormy night Sir Hugo and some of his wicked
companions kidnapped a young woman, the
daughter of a local farmer. Sir Hugo locked
her up in Baskerville Hall, but she managed to
climb down from a window and escape across
the moor. Mad with rage, Sir Hugo released his
pack of hunting dogs and galloped after her.'

'What about his friends?' I asked. 'Did they
not try to stop Sir Hugo?'

'They rode after him,' our visitor
continued, 'but when they reached Sir Hugo

a terrible sight met their eyes. The poor girl lay between two ancient stones, struck dead with fear. Nearby stood a great, black beast, shaped like a hound, yet larger than any hound ever seen by human eyes. The foul creature had torn the throat out of Hugo Baskerville. As it turned its blazing eyes and dripping jaws upon them, the three shrieked with fear and rode for dear life, still screaming, across the moor. And from that day onwards, many of the Baskerville family have suffered sudden and unexplained deaths.'

'That is an interesting story – for someone who collects fairy-tales!' Holmes remarked.

Dr Mortimer took a newspaper cutting from his jacket pocket. 'A fairy-tale perhaps, Mr

Holmes. But here is something more recent. This report from the *Devon County Chronicle*, dated June 14th this year, gives the facts about the death of Sir Charles Baskerville which occurred just a few days before.'

Sudden Death of Sir Charles Baskerville

Sir Charles Baskerville was found dead at his home, Baskerville Hall, on 4th June. He was the owner of the Baskerville Estate, on Dartmoor.

During the recent inquest into this tragic event, the jury was told that on that night Sir Charles had gone for his usual evening walk down the famous Yew Alley drive of Baskerville Hall. When he had not returned by midnight, his butler, Barrymore, went to look for him. Barrymore discovered Sir Charles' dead body at the end of the drive and sent for Dr Mortimer. At the inquest, Dr Mortimer told the jury that Sir Charles had been suffering from heart disease for some time. Dr Mortimer explained that when he had examined the body, Sir Charles' face had been wildly distorted, as if he had suffered painful heart failure. No other signs of violence were found on the body. The inquest decided that death had been caused by a severe heart attack.

The Baskerville Estate will be inherited by Mr Henry Baskerville, who now lives in Canada, and is the son of Sir Charles Baskerville's younger brother. The new baronet, Mr Henry (now Sir Henry) Baskerville has been informed and is travelling to England.

Dr Mortimer refolded his cutting and put it back in his pocket.

'Those are the public facts, Mr Holmes, in connection with the death of Sir Charles Baskerville.'

'Then let me have the private ones,' replied Holmes.

Dr Mortimer turned towards us and began his story. 'I was a close friend of Sir Charles Baskerville. There are very few other educated people in that part of the moor, apart from Mr Stapleton, the scientist and butterfly collector, who lives close by. For some time I had noticed that Sir Charles was becoming strained and nervous. He took the ancient legend very seriously, and was convinced that some dreadful fate hung over his family.

'On the night of Sir Charles' death the butler, Barrymore, who had discovered the body, sent Perkins the groom on horseback to find me. When I got to Baskerville Hall I found Sir Charles lying dead on the path. His face was convulsed and twisted with horror. There was certainly no physical injury of any kind. But one false statement was made by Barrymore at the inquest. He said that there were no other traces upon the ground round the body. He did not observe any. However, I did – a short distance off, but fresh and clear.'

'Footprints?' asked Holmes.

'Footprints.'

'A man's or a woman's?'

Dr Mortimer looked strangely at us for an instant, and his voice sank almost to a whisper as he answered:

'Mr Holmes, they were the footprints of a gigantic hound!'

I confess that at these words a shudder passed through me.

'Surely, Sir, you do not believe that there can have been a supernatural explanation for Sir Charles Baskerville's death?' I asked Dr Mortimer.

'I am not sure what to believe, Dr Watson. Sir Charles died of a painful heart attack. But I do know that before the terrible event occurred several people had seen a creature upon the moor which corresponds with this Baskerville demon, and which could not possibly be any animal known to science. They all agreed that it was a huge creature, luminous, ghastly, and spectral.'

Holmes laughed. 'Perhaps you should consult a clergyman rather than a detective!'

'Perhaps,' Dr Mortimer replied. 'However, I am meeting Sir Henry Baskerville, the new baronet, this afternoon. He has just arrived in London from Canada. I would be most grateful if I could bring Sir Henry to meet with you tomorrow morning. We will both welcome your advice.'

Dr Mortimer and Sir Henry arrived at our rooms in 221b Baker Street the next morning. Sir Henry Baskerville was a small, alert, dark-eyed man, about thirty years of age, very sturdily built, with thick black eyebrows and a strong, determined face. He wore a dark red tweed suit and had the

weather-beaten appearance of someone who has spent a lot of time outdoors.

'Congratulations on your inheritance, Sir Henry,' said Holmes. 'I take it there were no other family members with a claim to the Baskerville Estate?'

'None, Mr Holmes. I am the last living member of the Baskerville family. Sir Charles was the eldest of three brothers. The second brother, my father, died when I was a boy. Sir Charles Baskerville's youngest brother, Roger Baskerville, would have been left the estate if he had lived. However, he died in South America some years ago. He had no children.'

'Has Dr Mortimer told you about the legend of the hound, and the mysterious footprints found by Sir Charles's body?' Holmes asked.

'He has, Sir. And I must tell you that there is no devil in hell, Mr Holmes, and no man on earth who can prevent me moving to Baskerville Hall and claiming my inheritance.'

Holmes nodded. 'I admire your courage, but nevertheless, I would be easier in my mind if you agreed to do two things. Firstly, to promise me that you will allow my colleague Dr Watson to accompany you and Dr Mortimer to Baskerville Hall. I cannot at present leave London as there are urgent matters for me to attend to here, but Watson will send me regular reports. And secondly, to promise that you will avoid the moor in the hours of darkness.'

Sir Henry agreed to Holmes' requests, and I arranged to meet him and Dr Mortimer at the station the next day.

As the baronet was leaving our rooms, he

said with a chuckle. 'By the way, Mr Holmes, since you are a famous detective, perhaps you could solve the problem of my missing black boot! One of the pair has disappeared from my hotel room. I cannot imagine what use a single boot will be to the thief!'

Holmes looked thoughtful, but said nothing.

The following day I met Sir Henry Baskerville and Dr Mortimer at the railway station, and we had a swift and pleasant journey down to Devonshire.

We left the train at a small country station on the edge of the moor, and continued our journey in a horse-drawn wagon. The green fields and fertile countryside soon gave way to a harsher landscape.

'There is your first sight of Dartmoor, Sir Henry,' said Dr Mortimer.

In front of us lay the huge expanse of the moor, grey and gloomy, with distant views of jagged and sinister hills. It was like some fantastic land seen in a dream. A cold wind swept down from it, and the road in front of us grew bleaker and wilder.

As we passed a rocky mound beside the road, we saw a group of men dressed in uniforms and carrying rifles. They were standing on the outcrop and looking intently out across the moor. Dr Mortimer stopped the wagon next to them.

'Do continue your journey, gentlemen,' said one of them. 'We are searching for a dangerous convict who has escaped from Dartmoor Prison – Selden, the Notting Hill murderer. He has been missing for some days now and cannot survive much longer on the moor without food or shelter.'

Soon afterwards we reached Baskerville Hall, an ancient stone house with ivy-covered walls and tall chimney pots. We were greeted by Barrymore, the butler, and his wife, the housekeeper. After Dr Mortimer drove off in the wagon to his own home nearby, Barrymore left us to warm our hands in front of a blazing log fire in the sitting room, while he and his wife prepared our evening meal.

'Dr Watson, I am sure you will not mind if I spend tomorrow morning discussing estate business with Barrymore,' Sir Henry said.

I told Sir Henry that I would be happy to explore the surrounding countryside while he was busy with his new duties.

After breakfast, Sir Henry gave Barrymore a parcel of clothes he had worn in London and no longer needed. 'Now I am a country gentleman, I must try to look the part!' he said. 'I hope you enjoy your morning walk, Dr Watson.'

I left Baskerville Hall and the broad path down Yew Alley soon changed into a rough moorland track. As I passed through a gloomy valley between two rocky tors, a man ran towards me. He was small, slim, clean-shaven, fair-haired and lean jawed, between thirty and forty years of age, dressed in a grey suit and wearing a straw hat. He carried a green butterfly-net in one of his hands.

'Allow me to introduce myself, Dr Watson,' he said. 'I visited Dr Mortimer earlier today and he told me that you were staying at Baskerville Hall. My name is Stapleton. If you have time to walk with me to my home, Merripit House, my sister will be glad to meet you.'

I accepted Stapleton's kind invitation and walked with him along a narrow path through the rough heather. Close by I could see some bright green patches of lush grassland amongst the barren landscape.

'That looks like a fine place for a gallop!' I observed.

Stapleton shook his head. 'Others have thought so, and been killed for their mistake,' he answered. 'That is the great Grimpen Mire. It is a deadly swamp of liquid mud covered with green scum – and any person who steps into it will sink without trace. Follow this path very carefully, Doctor, and you will be safe.'

We had gone a little further upon our journey when a strange sound echoed across the moor. A long, low moan filled the whole air, yet it was impossible to say from whence it came.

'What is that?' I cried.

Stapleton looked at me with a curious expression on his face.

'Strange place, the moor!' said he.

'But what is it?'

'The local people say it is the Hound of the Baskervilles calling for its prey.'

I looked round, with a chill of fear in my heart, at the huge plain, mottled with the green patches. Nothing stirred over the vast expanse save a pair of ravens, which croaked loudly from a rocky tor behind us.

'You are an educated man. Surely you don't believe such nonsense as that?' said I. 'What do you think is the cause of so weird a sound?'

'Perhaps the sound of the bittern,' replied Stapleton. 'It is a very rare bird with a deep booming call – practically extinct in England now, but there may be some specimens left on the moor.'

I was not convinced by his explanation, and felt that perhaps Stapleton knew more than he was prepared to say.

As we came in site of Merripit House, the scientist suddenly reached for his net and set off at great pace across the moor. I could see that he was chasing after a colourful butterfly – no doubt a rare specimen. At the same time, the front door opened and a young woman ran towards me. I realised that this was Stapleton's sister, although she looked nothing like her brother. She was slim, elegant and tall, with an olive complexion and jet black hair. Her eyes were on her brother as she quickened her pace towards me.

'Go back!' she said. 'Go straight back to London, instantly.'

Before she could say more, Stapleton had returned.

Miss Stapleton turned to him, struggling to calm herself. 'I was just welcoming Sir Henry Baskerville to our home.'

'Madam, you are mistaken. I am not Sir Henry. I am Dr Watson, Sir Henry's friend,' I said.

Miss Stapleton looked worried and embarrassed at her mistake, but I said no more about her warning. Later, as I returned to Baskerville Hall, I wondered why she was so anxious for Sir Henry to leave. Did she have any information about the death of Sir Charles Baskerville, or the strange sounds heard on the moor? That evening I wrote a letter to Sherlock Holmes, who was still in London, telling him everything that had occurred. Would he be able to use his powers of deduction to discover the truth about these strange events?

Sir Henry Baskerville was soon introduced to the Stapletons, and over the next few days he visited them regularly. It was clear to me that the baronet was attracted to Stapleton's sister, and I felt that before long there might be a new Lady Baskerville living in the Hall.

One afternoon, Sir Henry returned from his visit to Merripit House, flustered and angry.

'Watson, I cannot understand it!' he said. 'As you know, I have become very attached to Miss Stapleton. Today, when for a short time I was walking alone with her on the moor, I told her that I wished her to be my wife. She in turn seemed frightened, and pleaded with me to leave Devonshire and return to London! When Stapleton joined us, I explained that I had proposed marriage to his sister. His response was to fly into a furious rage. He turned white with anger and hurled abuse at me. What can he possibly hold against me?

And why is Miss Stapleton so insistent that I leave Baskerville Hall? Surely my situation in life would make me a very suitable husband for her, if only she will accept me?'

I was not able to answer Sir Henry's questions, but I felt that there was something about Stapleton, and indeed his sister, that I had yet to discover. Later that day I wrote again to Sherlock Holmes, telling him what had taken place.

I am usually a sound sleeper, but some days later, troubled by strange dreams of the hound and the moor, I slept lightly. At about two o'clock in the morning I was woken by a step passing my room. I crept to my bedroom door and opened it carefully. A long black shadow was trailing down the corridor. It was thrown by a man who walked softly away from me with a candle in his hand. I could only see the outline, but his height told me that it was Barrymore. What secret task was he engaged in?

When the figure turned and went into one of the empty bedrooms at the end of the corridor, I quickly roused Sir Henry. It took but a moment to explain what I had observed, and for us to return to the room which Barrymore had entered. Slowly and silently we opened the door. Barrymore was standing in front of a window which overlooked the moor, candle in hand, moving it back and forth as if to send a signal. When we entered the room he turned round in shock and surprise.

Sir Henry demanded an immediate explanation, but Barrymore refused to give one.

'Don't ask me, Sir! Don't ask me! The secret is not mine to tell!' he cried.

Just as the baronet was threatening his servant with instant dismissal, Mrs Barrymore rushed into the room, her hair uncombed and her dressing gown hurriedly thrown over her night-clothes. Tearfully, she told us the reason for her husband's suspicious behaviour.

'He was doing it for me, Sir Henry – or rather for my brother – Selden, the convict.'

Mrs Barrymore explained that the escaped prisoner hiding on the moor was her younger brother. She and her husband had been supplying him with clothes and food, left outside at night after Selden had been given a signal from the window.

'I cannot blame you for standing by your own flesh and blood', said Sir Henry. 'I will not report your assistance to Selden – but do not expect me to help him avoid capture.'

As the Barrymores were leaving us, the butler turned towards Sir Henry. 'In return for your kindness, Sir, I can give you some information that may prove useful. Selden has told my wife that he is not the only man hiding out on the moor. Several times he has seen a tall figure, distant and indistinct, close to the circle of stone huts below Vixen Tor. No doubt the stranger is sheltering there.'

I resolved to search for the stranger alone, rather than risk any danger to Sir Henry. The following afternoon, as soon as I was sure that Sir Henry was busy with his estate business, I set off for the ancient settlement.

As I grew near to my destination, a mist gathered upon the farthest skyline, out of which jutted the fantastic shape of Vixen Tor. The barren scene, the sense of loneliness, and the mystery and urgency of my task, all struck a chill into my heart.

Down beneath me in a cleft of the hills lay the circle of old stone huts. In the middle there was one with the remains of a roof to give some protection against the weather. This must be the burrow in which the stranger lurked.

My nerves tingled with a sense of adventure as I approached the hut. Throwing away my cigarette, I closed my hand upon the butt of my revolver, and dashed inside. The place was empty, but a loaf of bread, some tinned food and a rough straw mattress showed that someone was living there. I lay in wait for a long time, until darkness began to fall over the moor. Finally, the clink of approaching footsteps against the stones on the path told me that the mysterious figure was drawing near.

'It is a fine evening, my dear Watson,' said a cheerful and well-known voice. 'I really think that you will be more comfortable outside than in.'

When I emerged I was amazed to see
Sherlock Holmes standing in front of me!

'How on earth did you know that I was
inside the hut?' I asked. 'And Holmes, what
the blazes are you doing here on the moor,
when I have been writing regularly to you in
London?'

Holmes smiled. 'The answer to your first
question is simple. When I saw the stub of
your favourite brand of cigarettes lying on
the path – thrown away, no doubt, when you

charged into the empty hut – I knew that Watson could not be far away! As for your second question, that requires a more detailed explanation.'

Holmes apologized for his deception. He told me that shortly after I had left London, he had followed me to Dartmoor in secret, so that he could carry out his investigations without being discovered.

'Your excellent reports have not been wasted, Watson – I arranged for your letters to be sent on to the village post office near Baskerville Hall, where I could collect them. Your description of the Stapletons and their actions instantly aroused my suspicions. I have since found out that Stapleton was in London when Sir Henry arrived from Canada, and was responsible for the mysterious theft of one of the baronet's black boots. Furthermore, I now know that Miss Stapleton is in fact not Stapleton's sister – she is his wife!'

'His wife!' I exclaimed. 'That would explain a great deal. But what is he after? What can he possibly have to gain from these sinister deceptions?'

'Never fear, Watson. My investigations are now almost complete. Stapleton is planning some deadly deed, and we will soon have the final proof – but listen!'

A terrible scream rang out from the depths of the moor. The frightful sound turned the blood to ice in my veins.

'Holmes!' I gasped. 'What is it? What does it mean?'

Again the agonized cry swept through the silence of the gathering dusk, louder and much nearer than before. And a new sound mingled with it, a deep baying note, musical and yet menacing.

'The hound!' cried Holmes. 'Come, Watson, come! Great heavens, if only we are not too late!'

Blindly we ran through the gloom, blundering against boulders, forcing our way through gorse bushes, panting up hills and rushing down slopes. We looked round eagerly, but the shadows were thick upon the moor, and nothing moved upon its dreary landscape.

As we got closer to the fearful sounds, we saw a ridge of rocks above us, ending in a steep cliff. On the stone-covered slope below lay a dark, still shape. When we reached it, the sight turned our hearts sick and faint within us – it was the body of Sir Henry Baskerville, his skull crushed by the fall! We both recognised that unusual dark red tweed suit. It was the very one which he had worn on the first morning that we had seen him in Baker Street.

'Why did Sir Henry risk his life by walking alone on the moor, after all our warnings?' I wondered.

Holmes stepped closer to the body and bent down to examine it. 'Believe me, Watson,

Stapleton will answer for this crime. I am now convinced that it is he who has brought the hound to the moor, in order to carry out these dreadful acts. Sir Charles and Sir Henry have both been murdered – one frightened to death by the creature, and one killed trying to escape it. But now we have to prove the connection between Stapleton and the beast ... '

Holmes' voice changed suddenly. I could not believe my eyes as he began jumping and shouting for joy.

'Watson! Watson! This man has a beard! Look at his face! This is not Sir Henry Baskerville, it is Selden, the escaped convict.'

It was clear to both of us what must have happened. When Sir Henry had given his old clothes to Barrymore, his wife passed them on to Selden as part of their plan to help him escape from the moor. Stapleton had used Sir Henry's stolen boot to put the hound on the scent of its victim, and the creature had killed the convict by mistake.

Holmes turned towards me. 'We will put Selden's body under this rocky ledge and leave it there until morning. I will inform the police at daybreak.'

'And what shall we tell Sir Henry when we get back to Baskerville Hall?' I asked.

'Say nothing to him about the baying of the hound.' Holmes replied. 'We will explain that Selden fell to his death by accident.

Sir Henry has been invited to dinner at the Stapletons' house tomorrow night, and it is best that he suspects nothing. That will give us our chance to prove Stapleton's guilt. And now, my dear Watson, I think we are both ready for our suppers.'

That evening, a grey mist rose from the moor and gathered in the grounds of the Hall. Sir Henry was very surprised when Sherlock Holmes asked him to visit the Stapletons alone.

'Trust me,' Holmes said. 'My instructions may seem strange, but it is vital that you follow them completely. I can promise that you will come to no harm. Ask Perkins to drive you to Merripit House in the horse and trap. When you arrive, send Perkins back to Baskerville Hall, and be sure to tell the Stapletons that you intend to walk home alone across the moor. Watson and I will stay here at Baskerville Hall and await your return.'

Sir Henry was puzzled, but agreed to do as Holmes asked. As the baronet left with Perkins, Holmes turned to me. 'We will follow him on foot in fifteen minutes. I have my revolver – be sure that you take yours also. I fear there is danger ahead of us tonight.'

When we reached Merripit House, Holmes and I concealed ourselves behind a mound of jagged rocks, about two hundred yards from the front door. We remained in hiding for several hours, waiting for Sir Henry to finish his meal and start his return journey.

The gathering mist swirled round us, and a huge lake of dense fog hung in the still air over Grimpen Mire nearby. Then a figure emerged from a side door – but it was Stapleton, not Sir Henry. He walked to a small hut near the side of the house, unlocked the door and returned to the house, leaving the shed door open. Was that a faint scuffling and panting noise I could hear?

Holmes turned towards me, his finger at his lips. 'Not long now, Watson! Be sure to stay silent until Sir Henry comes near.'

At that moment the front door opened. Sir Henry and Stapleton stood upon the threshold, outlined in the light from the doorway. There was no sign of Stapleton's wife as the two men said goodbye.

The fog on the path thickened as Sir Henry walked towards our hiding place. Once again, I could hear heavy panting – and the swift patter of footsteps. Sir Henry glanced over his shoulder and began running towards us. As he did so, a terrifying creature emerged from the fog behind him. Holmes and I stood frozen in horror.

A hound it was, an enormous coal-black hound, but not such a hound as mortal eyes have ever seen. Fire burst from its open mouth, its eyes glowed with a smouldering glare, its muzzle and throat were outlined in flickering flame. Never in the delirious dream of a disordered brain could anything more savage, more appalling, more hellish be conceived than that dark form and savage face which broke upon us out of the wall of fog.

As the hound passed us, close on Sir Henry's heels, we came to our senses. Both our revolvers fired at close range, and the beast screamed out as it fell dead to the ground.

'That is no phantom creature!' Holmes cried.

Far away on the path we saw Sir Henry looking back, his face white in the moonlight, his hands raised in horror, glaring helplessly at the frightful thing which had been hunting him down.

'Good grief!' the baronet whispered. 'What was it? What, in heaven's name, was it?'

'It's dead, whatever it is,' said Holmes. 'We've laid the family ghost once and forever.'

Even now in the stillness of death, the huge jaws seemed to be dripping with a bluish flame and the small, deep-set eyes were ringed with fire. I placed my hand upon the glowing muzzle, and as I held them up my own fingers smouldered and gleamed in the darkness.

'Phosphorus,' I said. 'Some compound of the substance has been rubbed into this poor creature's fur to make it glow in the dark. Huge though it is, it looks half starved. Stapleton must have released it from the hut and set it on its prey.'

Leaving the baronet to recover from his fearful experience, we rushed into the house, but as we expected, Stapleton had vanished. We discovered his wife upstairs in one of the bedrooms, bound and gagged.

She told us that she had long suspected that her husband was responsible for the death of Sir Charles, and was plotting to murder Sir Henry, but had been kept in fear for her life.

'My husband threatened to kill me if I gave him away – and I believed him,' she told us. 'I tried to warn Sir Henry, but my husband was always close by. Then this evening I told him I would stay silent no more. His response was to lock me away and tell Sir Henry that I was unwell and could not dine with them tonight. But I can tell you where he will have fled. At the centre of Grimpen Mire – reached by a dangerous path – is a small island where he kept his hound well hidden. He will no doubt try to escape there.'

The dense fog made any search useless that night, so it was not until the next morning that we followed the twisting and indistinct path that led through Grimpen Mire. It would have been impossible to have passed over it safely the night

before. No trace of Stapleton was ever found –
only Sir Henry's stolen boot, used to put the
hound on the scent of its victim, and dropped
by the fugitive as he stumbled to his own
terrible death in the mire.

Later that day, Holmes met again with
Stapleton's wife, and with her help he put
together the remaining pieces of the puzzle.
When he joined me at Baskerville Hall,
Holmes explained all that he had discovered.

'As I suspected, Stapleton had been living
here under a false name. He was, in fact, Jack
Baskerville, the son of Roger Baskerville, Sir
Charles' youngest brother. He had discovered

that only Sir Charles and Henry Baskerville stood between him and the valuable estate.'

'But Sir Henry told us that Roger Baskerville had no children,' I said.

'Sir Henry was mistaken,' Holmes replied. 'When Roger Baskerville's son found out about the legend of the hound, he realised that here was the chance to dispose of his two relatives and inherit a fortune. He moved from South America to Dartmoor, and forced his wife to go with him. And to avoid detection he changed his name to Stapleton. On the way, he stopped in London to buy the biggest and fiercest dog he could find. Jack Baskerville knew that Sir Charles had a weak heart, and that the sight of such a frightening creature would probably scare him to death. Sir Henry's fate would have been far worse – the hound was half-starved and would have killed the baronet if it had lived.'

'But why pretend that his wife was his sister?' I asked.

Holmes smiled. 'No doubt he felt that Sir Henry would be much more likely to visit Merripit House with the attractive "Miss Stapleton" living there.'

I moved to the window and looked out over the barren landscape of the moor. 'Using a luminous chemical to transform his savage dog into a glowing, spectral hound was a stroke of genius,' I said.

'Indeed. The man was both wicked and clever – a deadly combination. But evil does not go unpunished in this world. Jack Baskerville lies beneath Grimpen Mire, and has paid for his crimes. And now, as our work in Devonshire is done, let us return to London on the afternoon train. After our dangerous adventure, my dear Watson, I think we deserve a pleasant evening. I suggest dinner at Marcini's restaurant, and then the opera!'

TAKING THINGS FURTHER

The real read

This *Real Reads* version of *The Hound of the Baskervilles* is a retelling of Arthur Conan Doyle's famous original work. If you would like to read the full story, many complete editions are available, from bargain paperbacks to beautiful hardbacks. You should be able to find a copy in your local library, book shop or charity shop.

Filling in the spaces

The loss of so many of Conan Doyle's original words is a sad but necessary part of the shortening process. We have had to make some difficult decisions, omitting subplots and details, some important, some less so, but all interesting. We have also, at times, taken the liberty of combining two events into one, or of giving a character words or actions that originally belong to another. The points below will fill in some of the gaps, but nothing can beat the original.

- After Sir Henry Baskerville arrives in London, he receives a mysterious letter telling him to keep away from the moor. Later on, Sherlock Holmes is able to prove that the letter was sent by Miss Stapleton.

- When Sir Henry and Dr Watson find out that Barrymore is signalling to the escaped convict, Selden, they go out onto the moor. They see Selden but are unable to catch him.

- Dr Watson is shown where to find the strange man on the moor by Mr Frankland, an eccentric gentleman who amuses himself by taking out court cases against his neighbours.

- Barrymore reveals that Sir Charles Baskerville had arranged to meet someone in Yew Alley on the night of his death. This person wrote Sir Charles a note signed 'LL'. Holmes and Watson discover that 'LL' is Laura Lyons, Mr Frankland's daughter. They also find out that Stapleton tricked Laura Lyons into making the appointment, so that he could release the hound when Sir Charles was nearby.

• When Holmes and Watson find an old picture of Sir Hugo Baskerville, they see that it looks very like Stapleton – this gives them an important clue.

• Holmes arranges for Inspector Lestrade to come down to Devonshire from London. Lestrade helps Holmes and Watson when they follow Sir Henry to Merripit House.

• The final scene in the original story takes place in London, where Holmes and Watson discuss the case after they have returned from the moor. They raise a tricky question: if Stapleton had got rid of Sir Henry, how could he have claimed the estate (as Jack Baskerville) without being recognised? Holmes suggests that Stapleton might have gone back to South America to claim his inheritance, without showing his face again on the moor.

Back in time

Late-Victorian Britain was a land of contrasts. One of these contrasts was between London and the other big cities – with their bright gas lights, busy streets, shops, offices, and theatres – and the isolated countryside. In *The Hound of the Baskervilles* (set in 1887 and published in 1901) Dr Watson can travel from London to Dartmoor by steam train in just a few hours, but when he arrives he has to follow rough paths on foot or by horse and cart. The cosy rooms at 221b Baker Street are replaced by a wild, gloomy and haunting landscape which would have thrilled those who read the story when it was first published, and still excites us today. Although modern Dartmoor is a much tamer place, Conan Doyle's skills as a story teller can take us back to the days when there were no tarmac roads, cars or mobile phones to help the lonely traveller, and when even the richest person would use a flickering candle to light their way to bed.

Another contrast of the time was between the Victorians' great advances in science and technology and their continued fascination by myths, legends and folklore. Conan Doyle would have heard many traditional tales of ghostly black dogs and other phantom creatures. One of the things that makes *The Hound of the Baskervilles* such a gripping story is that the reader is never quite sure, until the end, whether the hound is real or supernatural! Although Sherlock Holmes seems to think that such legends are 'fairy-tales', Dr Mortimer – himself a man of science – and the others are not so certain. Further scientific progress has not stopped the modern reader from sharing, and enjoying, the spine-tingling encounters with a beast that may not be of this world.

Finding out more

We recommend the following books, websites and films to gain a greater understanding of Sir Arthur Conan Doyle and the world he lived in.

Books

• Sir Arthur Conan Doyle, *The Adventures of Sherlock Holmes*, Penguin Popular Classics, 1994. A selection of twelve Sherlock Holmes stories.

• Sir Arthur Conan Doyle, *The Lost World*, Penguin Red Classics, 2007.

• John Dickenson Carr, *The Life of Sir Arthur Conan Doyle*, Carrol & Graf, 2003.

• Terry Deary, *Vile Victorians* (Horrible Histories) Scholastic, 1994.

• Ann Kramer, *Victorians* (Eyewitness Guides), Dorling Kindersley, 1998.

Websites

- www.siracd.com

Lots of information about the life and work of Sir Arthur Conan Doyle, including the Sherlock Holmes stories.

- www.221bakerstreet.org

A website with forty-eight Sherlock Holmes stories which are no longer 'in copyright' (that is, owned by anyone) and can therefore be legally downloaded or read on screen. There are also some original pictures, and other interesting things such as a map of 221b Baker Street.

- www.victorianweb.org

A good site to find out more about Victorian times – including writers, other famous people and everyday life.

- www.bbc.co.uk/history/british/victorians

The BBC's website about Victorian Britain, with a wide range of information and activities.

Films

The Hound of the Baskervilles (1959), Hammer Films, directed by Terence Fisher.

The Hound of the Baskervilles (1965), BBC, directed by Graham Evans.

If you are able to watch both of these, it is interesting to see the different ways in which each tackles the making of a film version.

Food for thought

Here are a few things to think about if you are reading *The Hound of the Baskervilles* alone, or ideas for discussion if you are reading it with friends.

In retelling *The Hound of the Baskervilles* we have tried to recreate, as accurately as possible, Arthur Conan Doyle's original plot and characters. We have also tried to imitate aspects of his style. Remember, however, that this is not the original work; thinking about the points below, therefore, can help you to begin to understand Arthur Conan Doyle's craft.

To move forward from here, turn to the full-length version of *The Hound of the Baskervilles* and lose yourself in his exciting and imaginative story.

Starting points

- In film versions of this story, Dr Watson is sometimes shown as a rather silly and unintelligent character. What do you think of Dr Watson?

- Can you find examples which show Sherlock Holmes' great skill in gaining a lot of information from small, everyday details?

- *The Hound of the Baskervilles* mentions some things early on which turn out to be very important clues later in the book. Can you find some examples?

- What does the story gain from being set on Dartmoor?

- How does the author make us think that the hound might be a supernatural creature?

Themes

What do you think Conan Doyle is saying about the following themes in *The Hound of the Baskervilles*?

- belief in the supernatural
- retribution – the consequences of bad deeds
- courage in the face of the unknown
- the influence of landscape

Style

Can you find paragraphs containing examples of the following?

- descriptions of settings or scenery which contribute to the tension and atmosphere of the story
- descriptions of the appearance of characters which help the reader to picture them very clearly
- vivid or dramatic speech
- a document or report written in a different style to the rest of the story, to add variety and realism

Look closely at how these paragraphs are written. What do you notice? Can you write a paragraph in the same style?